To my daughters Sarah and Hannah, who always inspire me to look for the Gertrude's and Lily Fa Lo's in life.

... Tim

In memory of Dennis, my biggest fan and patron. I only wish I could have finished in time to place a copy in your hands.

... Jess

THE ILLUSTRATIONS IN THIS BOOK WERE DONE IN ACRYLIC PAINT.
THE DISPLAY TYPE IS CHINESE ROCKS.
THE TEXT TYPE IS A MIX OF CHINESE ROCKS AND CABIN CONDENSED BOLD.

ISBN: 978-0692211731

FIRST EDITION
DESIGNED BY JESS BECHTELHEIMER

DOODLEHAUS BOOKS
LAKE TAHOE, USA

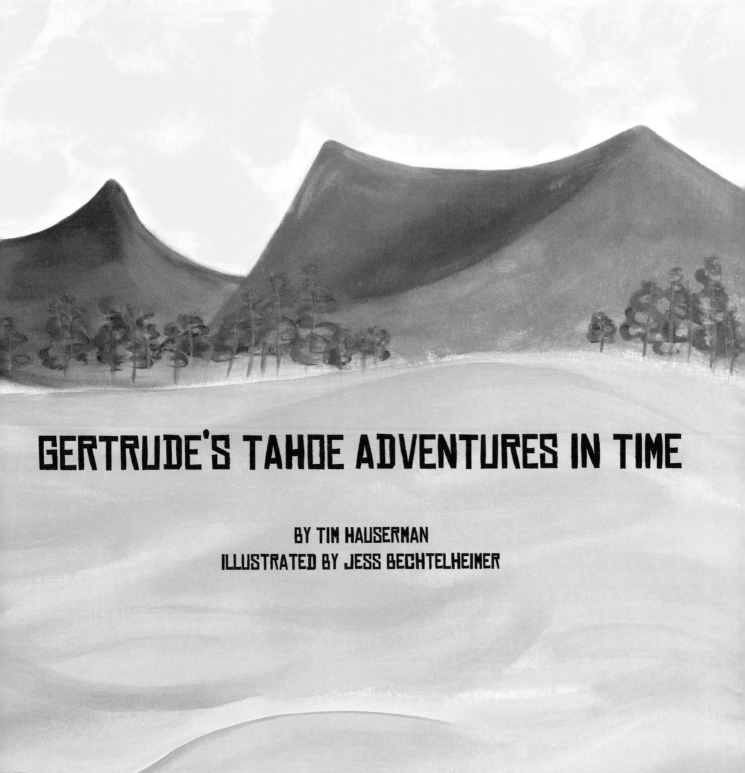

# GERTRUDE'S TAHOE ADVENTURES IN TIME

### BY TIM HAUSERMAN
### ILLUSTRATED BY JESS BECHTELHEIMER

**Gertrude** lay back on the smooth rock and let her toes tickle the water of the deep blue lake. She gazed at the high mountains covered in snow, watched the sailboat gently blow across the lake, then smiled and said, "I am so lucky to live here!"

She jumped up happily and skipped across the beach towards her tent, but tripped on a rock and fell to the ground. She stood up, dusted herself off and noticed that the offending rock was obsidian: big, black and shiny like a piece of glass.

Gertrude rubbed her hands on the smooth surface of the rock and suddenly an Indian maiden appeared. She was dressed in deerskin pants and colorful feathers, with flowers in her long dark hair. Gertrude thought she was the most beautiful woman in the world.

The maiden stretched her arms to the sky, groaned loudly, then smiled at Gertrude and said, "Whew...have you ever been stuck in a rock for one hundred years? While I can tell you, it's not fun."

Gertrude's eyes were as big as ping-pong balls and her mouth was as wide as the Truckee River... It took her a moment to get up the courage to speak, but then she said, "My name is Gertrude... wahh...what's your name?"

"My name is Lily Fa Lo. And since you have ended my curse I want to give you a big hug and tonight while you are sleeping I will give you a great gift."

The maiden enveloped her in her warm, soft, strong arms and Gertrude felt happy and loved. Lily Fa Lo laughed and skipped away, stopping every few seconds to jump up and cheer, "I'm free, I'm free..."

Just before she disappeared behind a boulder Lily Fa Lo said, "See you tonight."

That night Gertrude listened to the wind blowing in the trees, and to the sound of the waves on the beach, but she couldn't sleep. It was like Christmas Eve. She knew she had to go to sleep, but she was just too excited, she wanted to know what the gift would be, she just knew it was going to be special. Finally, her eyes closed and then...

Lily Fa Lo gently took Gertrude's hand and said, "Tonight we are going to travel through the history of your home from the time before there was a Lake Tahoe, to what it is like today."

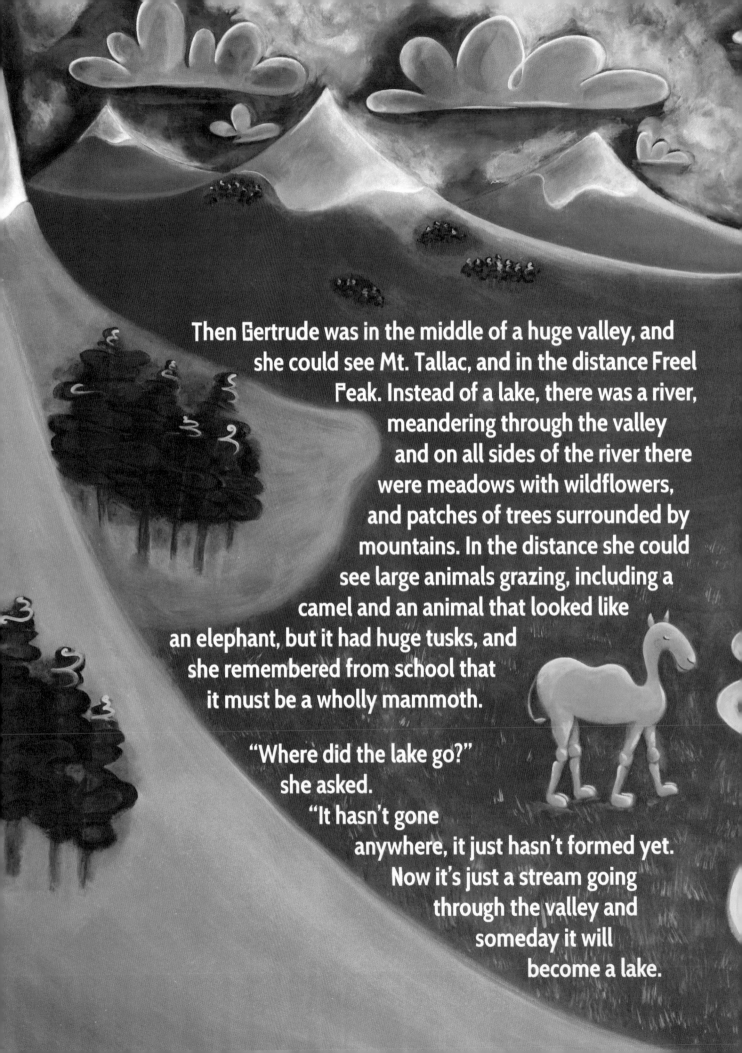

Then Gertrude was in the middle of a huge valley, and she could see Mt. Tallac, and in the distance Freel Peak. Instead of a lake, there was a river, meandering through the valley and on all sides of the river there were meadows with wildflowers, and patches of trees surrounded by mountains. In the distance she could see large animals grazing, including a camel and an animal that looked like an elephant, but it had huge tusks, and she remembered from school that it must be a wholly mammoth.

"Where did the lake go?" she asked.
"It hasn't gone anywhere, it just hasn't formed yet. Now it's just a stream going through the valley and someday it will become a lake.

We only
have a few hours.
We gotta keep things
moving along. Let me show
you how the lake was formed?"

Lily Fa Lo
told her to shut
her eyes as she gently
took Gertrude's shoulders
and spun her around in a circle
three times. As Gertrude opened
her eyes, she saw rivers of red lava
pouring out of a mountain followed
by a wave of steam where the lava
met the water. There was loud
rumbling and crashing.

Lily Fa Lo looked at her and said,
"All that lava is coming from the
mountain you now call Pluto."

Holding hands together they flew through the sky and soon they could see a lake. It was just a small lake now, but Gertrude could see that the lava had blocked the exit, and water from the river was backing up and slowly filling up the lake.

"Will that little lake become Lake Tahoe?" she asked.

"It will take many lifetimes, but every year it will get bigger until it is over 1500 feet deep."

Lily Fa Lo then spun her around in a circle three
times again, and they were up in the air looking down on
what was now a huge lake, but only a bit in the middle was
blue, the rest was all white.  It was snowing, and in the
mountains around the lake there was deep snow.

Then Gertrude realized that the lake was not only big, it was much bigger than Tahoe is now. "Wow" Gertrude said. "Why is the lake so big?" "That is because the volcano has blocked the Truckee River. But wait and you will see..."

Just then there was a noise, louder than anything Gertrude had ever heard, and Lily Fa Lo, pointed and yelled, "LOOK! OVER THERE!"

A wall of water and broken ice was rushing down the Truckee River, taking boulders as big as houses with it in a churning mass of water. Then it started to roar less and Gertrude noticed that the lake was about the same size as it is now.

"Is the lake like it is now?"
Gertrude asked.
"Closer, but not quite yet...
        watch..."

Then Gertrude could hear a loud, crunching and squeaking noise and then Lily Fa Lo gently grasped her hand and they were flying again. They flew over the lake, and Lily Fa Lo pointed down, "See right there...that will be Emerald Bay. There are big glaciers scouring out the valley that will become the lake. And look over there that will be Fallen Leaf Lake."

Then the maiden told Gertrude to shut her eyes and it was silent again, she opened her eyes and saw Lake Tahoe. But there were no houses or roads or buildings...but there were a few people...people dressed like Lily Fa Lo. They were fishing along the shore of the lake, and gathering nuts from the pine trees.

"Look, let's go visit," said Lily Fa Lo and they flew down and hovered over a women holding a small baby. Lily Fa Lo giggled and said, "Do you recognize that beautiful baby?"
Gertrude looked up at her, grinned and said, "Is that you?"
"I was pretty cute, eh?"
"You were cute...what happened?" she said with a smile. Then added, "So what was your life like?"
"I played in the trees, swam in the lake, gathered nuts and went fishing. Then in the winter we all would go to the warmer place to the east to escape the winter snows...it was a great life."
"What happened?"
"I can't tell you, it would break the spell," she said. Then she quickly grabbed her hand and said, "Let's go...we have to see when the white man came..."

Gertrude was afraid because they flew fast and then they were in the Nevada desert. "Where are we?" She asked.

"We are above Virginia City...see all the people down there, they are building mines, digging up silver...Now let's go back to the lake..."

Then they were above the lake and there was smoke and dust from railroad cars, and the sounds of saws as many trees were being cut down.
"Why are they cutting down so many trees?"
"To build the houses around the mines and tunnels inside the mines. By the time they are done, most of the trees in Tahoe will be cut...Most of my people have left, or you would see us crying..." Lily Fa Lo said, with a few tears coming down her cheeks.

Then Lily Fa Lo perked up and said, "Shut your eyes again...we are running out of time and there is still much for you to see."

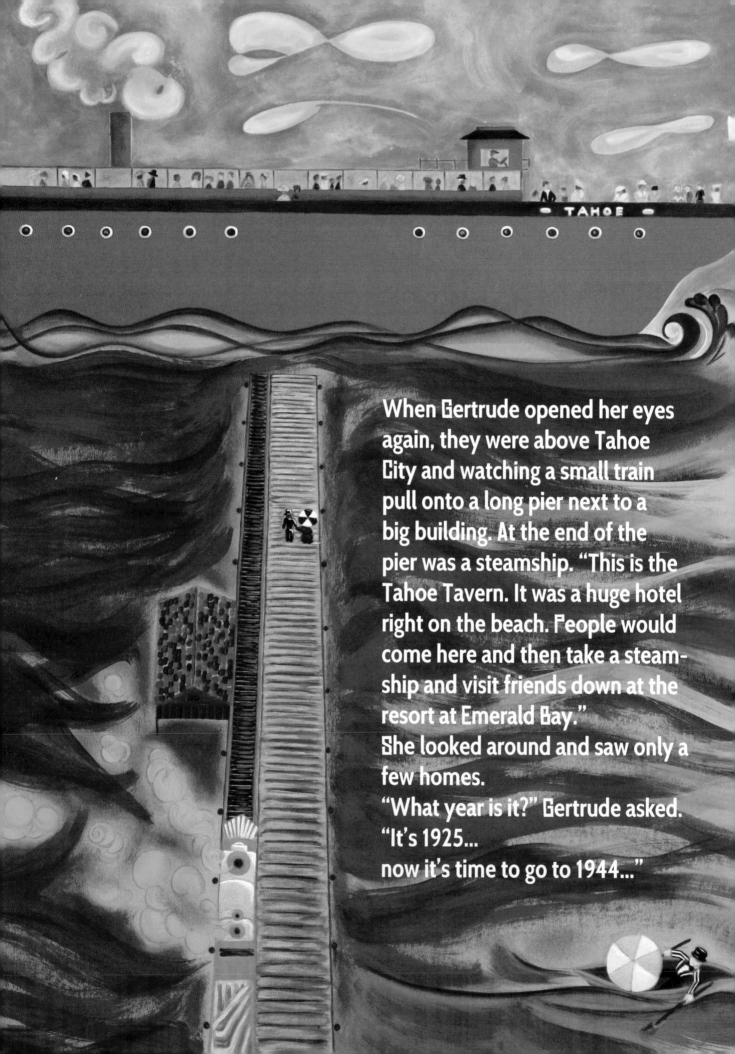

When Gertrude opened her eyes again, they were above Tahoe City and watching a small train pull onto a long pier next to a big building. At the end of the pier was a steamship. "This is the Tahoe Tavern. It was a huge hotel right on the beach. People would come here and then take a steamship and visit friends down at the resort at Emerald Bay."

She looked around and saw only a few homes.

"What year is it?" Gertrude asked.

"It's 1925...

now it's time to go to 1944..."

And they were flying above a big new hotel called Wagon Wheel Saloon. "This was the first gambling casino...then more followed along with lots of people to visit and to live here...now is when things are really starting to grow."

Then she grabbed her hand again and they were flying by an
Olympic flame and watching skiers race down a mountain.
"I know...this is the 1960 Winter Olympics in Squaw Valley!"
Gertrude said excitedly.
"My Grandparents were there...they told me all about it."

Then they flew again and Gertrude watched a crowd of people in her town sitting on the beach. "Hey, that was last week, when we went to the concert...can I see myself?"

"Sorry Gertrude, there isn't time...it's almost time to wake up...but if you want to see me again, just say Lily Fa Lo three times and I will be by your side."

"But I don't want you to leave me... where are you going?"

Lily Fa Lo stopped, touched her head quickly and said. "I am free once again to go back to my people. They can't see me, but I can live next to them, watch them and do what they are doing...and then when you call me, I will come visit you again...I am so grateful for you, because now I can see what is happening to the people I love... and I will watch you and be there with you when you need me."

Gertrude stirred from her sleep, as the sun came above the high mountains, her face lit up in bright gold. She stretched, smiled and thought of Lily Fa Lo.

Later that summer, Gertrude went hiking along the shores of Lake Tahoe and was sitting by herself at the entrance to Emerald Bay. She looked up at Mt. Tallac and Maggie's Peaks and quietly said, "Lily Fa Lo"....
"Lily Fa Lo" then again louder, "Lily Fa Lo!!" All of a sudden the maiden was sitting beside her.
"Hey Gertrude.  Isn't Tallac beautiful today?...you want to see what it looked like a million years ago...."

And they held hands and disappeared.

**TIM HAUSERMAN**

Tim Hauserman wrote Tahoe Rim Trail:
The official guide for hikers, mountain
bikers and equestrians; Monsters in the
Woods: Backpacking with Children; and
Cross-Country Skiing in the Sierra Nevada.
He writes for food and shelter, and for a variety
of magazines, newspapers and business blogs.

Tim teaches cross-country skiing and directs the Strider-Gliders
after school program at Tahoe Cross-Country Ski Area in Tahoe City, CA.
A nearly lifelong North Tahoe resident, in addition to cross-country skiing
Tim loves to road and mountain bike, hike and kayak. He also occasionally
takes a lesson in humility by attending a yoga class.

Jess spent her childhood drawing, hand sewing doll clothes, making miniature books that she wrote and illustrated herself, sculpting miniatures from clay, painting, and repurposing ephemeral to turn her entire room into a "barbie land" (as she called it).

Putting all that creative energy to good use, Jess went on to graduate from Wichita State University with a BFA in graphic design.

Years later, she decided to hit the road and start focusing on painting. It was during that time she discovered and fell in love with Tahoe.... and, of course, snowboarding.

She continues to create and fill life up with all the things she loves: bicycles, thrift shopping, farmer's markets, experimental cooking, making new friends, traveling and exploring new places, climbing trees, dancing, and playing board games.

## JESS BECHTELHEIMER

She is so excited and proud to say, this is her first children's book!

Come share in her adventures at painting-on-the-road.blogspot.com.
Stroll through paintings, graphic design, and upcycled clothing and home décor at spunkidoodle.com.
Find Jess' newest creations in her online shop, spunkidoodle.etsy.com.

Made in the USA
San Bernardino, CA
16 July 2014